Me...

Emma Dodd

The world is big...

and I am small.

The world is fast...

and I am small.

The ocean is deep...

and I am small.

The mountains are steep...

and I am small.

The wind is **strong**... and I am small.

The winter is long... and I am small.

The sky is high...

and I am small.

The stars stretch far...

and I am small.

These things are big and long and deep,

and strong and high and far and steep...

and I am small.

But you are **big** and you are **kind**.
When I'm with you, I do not mind.

I may be **small**, but I can see
the biggest thing to you...

...is me!

A TEMPLAR BOOK

First published in the UK in 2010 by Templar Publishing,
this softback edition published in 2013 by Templar Publishing,
an imprint of The Templar Company Limited,
Deepdene Lodge, Deepdene Avenue, Dorking, Surrey, RH5 4AT
www.templarco.co.uk

1 3 5 7 9 10 8 6 4 2

ISBN-13: 978-1-84877-814-6

Printed in China